Rainbow Wings

Joanne Ryder

illustrated by Victor Lee

HarperCollinsPublishers

For Larry, who dreams and
soars with dragon wings
—J.R.

Rainbow Wings

Text copyright © 2000 by Joanne Ryder
Illustrations copyright © 2000 by Victor Lee
Printed in Hong Kong by South China Printing Company (1988) Ltd.

Library of Congress Cataloging-in-Publication Data
Ryder, Joanne.
Rainbow wings / Joanne Ryder; illustrated by Victor Lee.
p. cm.
Summary: Illustrations and poetic text describe the wings of an owl,
a hummingbird, a butterfly, an eagle, a bat, and other creatures
and their different experiences of flight.
ISBN 0-688-14128-5 (trade)—ISBN 0-688-14129-3 (library)
[1. Wings—Fiction. 2. Animal flight—Fiction. 3. Animals—Fiction.]
I. Lee, Victor, ill. II. Title. PZ7.R959 Rai 1999 [E]—dc21 98-47038
CIP AC
1 3 5 7 9 10 8 6 4 2
❖
First Edition

Rainbow Wings, Inc.

Seraphina Cat,
Proprietor

An all-night rain
washes skies clean,
makes them bright,
just right for flying.
In the morning
double rainbows
arch high above you,
and shimmering spiderwebs
dot the wet grass.
Tucked among them
you may find
a pale card trimmed
with pawprints sky blue—

Wishing for Wings?

Look under the rainbows.
We're waiting to help you
find the wings of your fancy.
All flying dreams welcome.
Just today, not tomorrow.

COME . . . GET YOUR WINGS!

Just under the rainbows
the Cloud Cart is waiting.
A winged cat is stirring
to greet you and purrs:
I'm so glad that you came.
Today's *purr*fect for flying.
Let me show you our wings
in all colors and sizes.
Let me tell you about them.
Please give them a trial.
You can look. You can touch.
You can dream your own dream.
Try one on, try them all.
We live by our motto:
Let the wings match the wearer.
The choice will be yours.
Take your time.

Try these on
for a moment.
They're top quality—
strong and silent.
Beat them gently and listen.
They're as quiet as snow.
They're best worn at night
when moonlight is low.
You won't leave a shadow.
You won't make a sound.
In the dark, you are almost
invisible, and no one will know
where you are, where you go,
as you seek, as you sail,
as you swoop to the ground.

If you live near the ocean,
test these fine water wings.
Sleek and smooth,
basic black,
they're always in style.
You'll slide through the water,
you'll fly through the sea,
diving deep, rising high,
paddling quick as can be.
Waterproof, watertight,
they won't stretch, shrink, or stain.
Guaranteed color safe
in all seas—warm or cold.
Wings so easy to care for!
Just shake and they'll dry,
then fold neatly away
if you travel on shore
for a grand holiday.

Please open carefully,
spread these wings wide.
They're so new,
they are soft.
Let them dry.
Soon they'll harden
and glow
bright as marigolds,
edged like stained glass.
These wings
are for dancing,
for floating
like leaves in a breeze.
They are summer
in all of its splendor—
brassy and bold.
Who would think
wings so lovely,
so fragile and fine,
could carry you
thousands of miles
when the weather
turns cold?

Gray wings
may seem plain,
but they'll make
you an acrobat.
These are quicksilver wings
that blur as they beat,
that buzz as you fly.
Like the swiftest stunt flyer,
you'll climb,
then you'll dive,
hover still,
flip around,
and fly upside down.
In the blink of an eye
you are here…
you are there.
In the blink of an eye
you are gone!

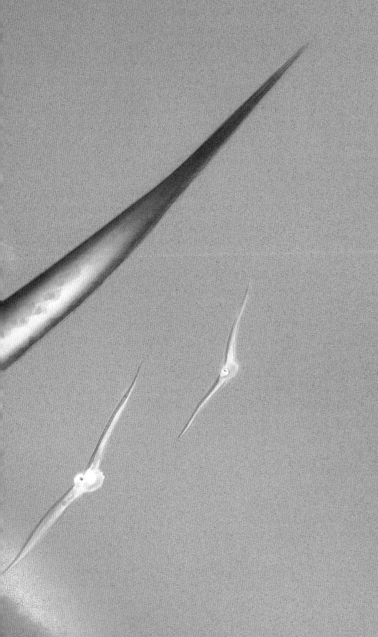

Our long narrow wings
are your ticket
to faraway seas.
You will glide
nearly touching the waves.
Then just turn,
find a breeze,
and you'll rise like a kite.
On the back of the wind
you ride free, you ride long,
soar into danger
and whirl through a storm.
Yet when the storms pass
and the sea's flat as glass,
you must wait
for a whisper of wind—
then you'll rise
to challenge the heavens,
brave sailor of skies.

If you like polka dots,
these wings might be you.
Black dots on red.
Red dots on black.
Take your pick.
Underneath,
you will find
a surprise—
dark wings, so thin
you can almost see
through them…
fine wings, so strong
they will carry you
home every time.
If you tuck them
and hide them
below your
bright covers,
they'll last
for a lifetime—
we promise!

These wings darted
over the dinosaurs
and never have gone
out of style.
Light and long,
they are clear
as fresh water,
yet shimmer
in sunlight.
Spread them wide—
do not fold
when you fly,
when you rest.
As you skim over ponds
and stop, standing still
in a space in the sky,
you'll discover
old wings are the best.

Want wings like an angel?
These are lovely and lush.
Lift them over your back
as you sail on a lake.
Oh! What an elegant
picture you make.
And musical too—
when you fly,
all will hear
whistling wings
when you're near.
These are wings
to bedazzle
with splendor and charm,
but mighty enough
to protect you from harm.
Let wings be your weapons
flapped fiercely at foes
who threaten and tease.
Beauty and strength—
who could ask
for wings finer than these.

Feathers need grooming
and constant attention.
You're not into molting
and preening? Okay.
Try these featherless wings,
wash and wear, easy care,
ever ready to take you
from night into day.
With webbed wings
leather smooth,
both agile and light,
you can zigzag,
win chases,
and race
through the night.

If you always look up
eyeing the mountaintop,
pick our high-country wings.
Spread them wide
and you'll glide in the air
warm and rising,
climbing spiraling staircases
no one can see,
over peaks, over mountains
till you soar ever higher,
till you soar wild and free.
Aloft in the heavens,
you waltz and you whirl
where only the boldest
adventurers go.
Oh, how daring to fly
rainbow high in the sky,
grandly viewing
the breathtaking
beauty below.

Made your choice?
Ah, how *purrfect*!
Those wings are just you.
I wish you smooth trips
and safe landings, my dears.

May you fly
where you wish
on your very own wings.
May they take you to places
found only in dreams.
May they carry you far,
bring you home safe and well,
full of wonders to share,
full of stories to tell.
Happy Wings!

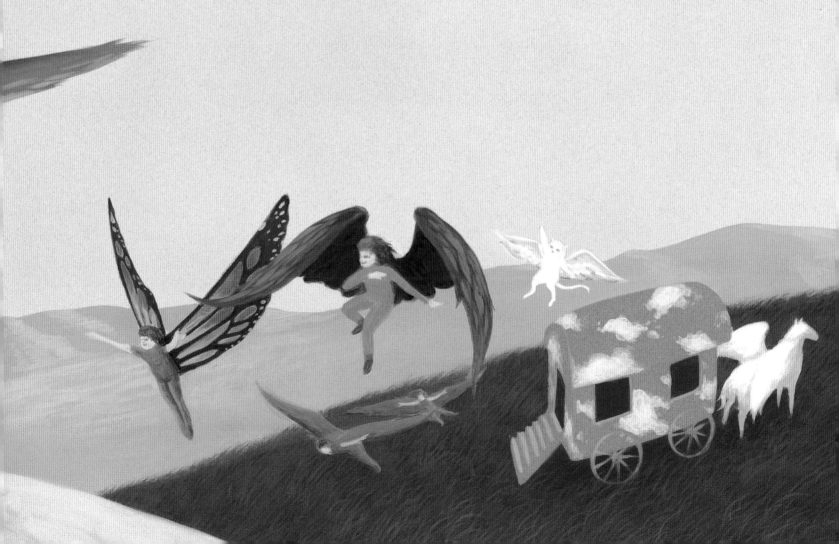

The *Wonder of Wings*

OWL wings are adapted for silent flight. As air flows over the smooth edges of most birds' wings in flight, it makes a noise. But soft comblike projections on owl wings disrupt airflow and muffle sound. Flying silently, an owl can better hear and locate prey and then approach it without warning.

PENGUINS cannot fly in the sky, but with their small sleek wings, they are well-suited for "flying" rapidly through the sea. Covered with very short feathers, penguin wings are flat, tapered, and stiff. These flipperlike wings enable penguins to swim up to 15 miles per hour underwater.

MONARCH BUTTERFLIES' orange-and-black wings help protect them. Their colors warn birds that the insects are poisonous to eat. Monarchs' wings carry them far—to their winter roosts in Mexico and California on a two-way migration of up to 3,000 miles.

HUMMINGBIRDS beat their wings so quickly—as often as 50 to 80 times per second—that the wings seem to blur. They are the only birds able to fly backward. Unlike other birds that walk or hop, hummingbirds always fly from one spot to another. When migrating, the ruby-throated hummingbird crosses the Gulf of Mexico, flying 500 miles without stopping to rest or eat.

ALBATROSSES can glide for hours without flapping their long narrow wings. Carried by the winds, some glide at speeds of 70 miles per hour. The wandering albatross has the longest wingspan of all flying birds. Its wings can span 11 feet from one wing tip to the other.

LADYBUGS are not bugs but beetles. Like other beetles, they have two pairs and two kinds of wings. When ladybugs are walking or resting, their thick, hard forewings cover and protect the delicate flying wings underneath. When ladybugs fly, the hard, spotted wings are held out of the way.

DRAGONFLIES flew over ancient swamps more than 250 million years ago. Prehistoric dragonflies were giants with wings spreading two feet wide. Today's dragonflies are smaller—with wingspans of several inches—but they still dazzle, darting forward at speeds of up to 100 body lengths per second.

MUTE SWANS are among the world's heaviest flying birds. They can weigh 30 pounds, and their whistling wings can span over seven feet.

BATS are the only mammals that truly can fly. Other mammals—like flying squirrels—can only glide from heights. Bat wings are leathery membranes that stretch from the bats' elongated fingers to their ankles.

GOLDEN EAGLES are majestic birds in appearance and flight. This "king of birds" soars with its broad wings outstretched, rising high on hot air currents called thermals. Spiraling aloft, it spots its prey below, then folds its wings and attacks, diving at speeds of over 100 miles per hour.